E
Nambiar

Still There?

A Little Zen for Little Ones™

By

Sanjay Nambiar

For Miya & Uma.

Special thanks to:
Priya Nambiar (for everything and so much more!), Nilesh Kapse, Vivek Pathare, Abhijeet Shrotri, Kavitha Dinesh, Kishor Vijay Nagar, Alyssa Williamson, Venu Alagh, and our parents and siblings.

Still There?

www.alittlezen.com

Edited by Priya Nambiar.
Illustrated by 3-Keys Graphics and Design.

First Edition | 10 9 8 7 6 5 4 3 2 1
ISBN 978-0-9838243-2-9
Library of Congress Control Number 2012902916

Printed in China.

This book will receive loving kindness from

_____

Two boys were playing on a schoolyard during lunchtime.

It was a beautiful day with a sunny sky and white puffy clouds.
A gentle breeze rustled the leaves on the trees.
It felt good to be outside.

They were running around and laughing with delight.

Suddenly, they heard a loud scream.

A girl in one of the older grades was yelling.

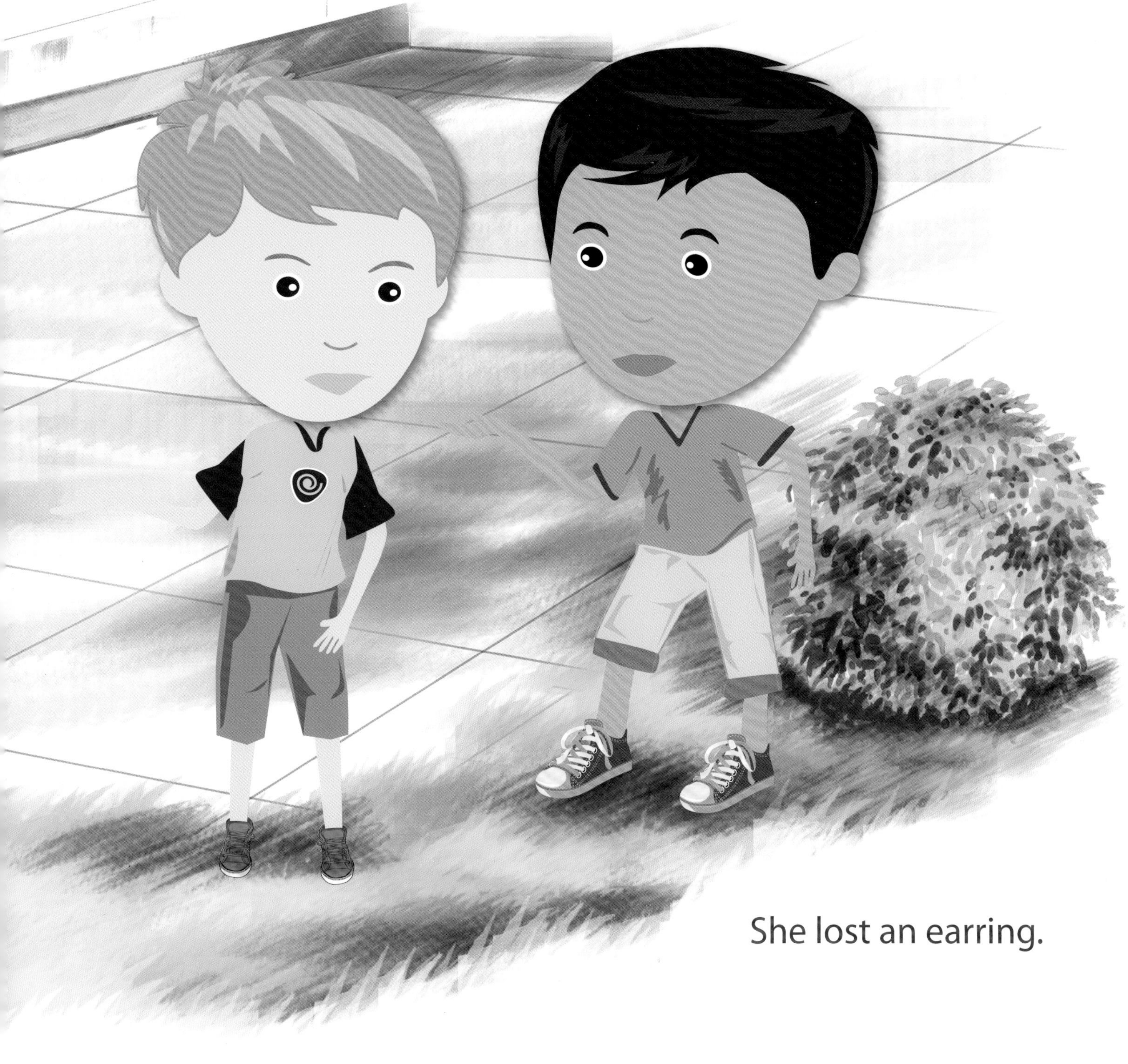

She lost an earring.

She shouted, "Where is my earring?
It's really expensive!
Somebody help me find it!"

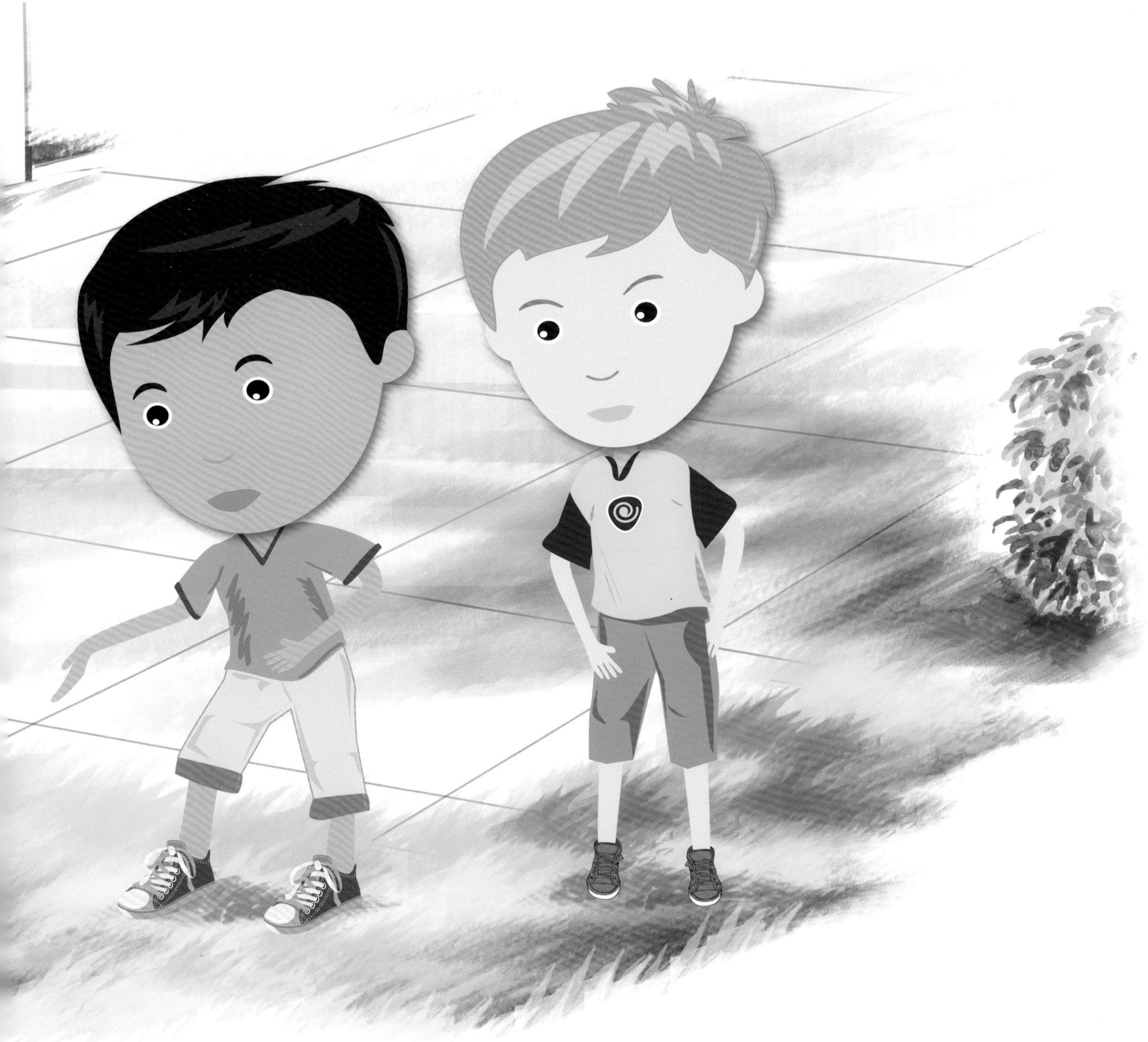

She was very angry.

She was very upset.

She was waving her hands.

She was stomping her feet.

But, she wasn't looking for her earring.

One of the two boys immediately started looking for the earring.
He got on his hands and knees and looked all around.

His hands got dirty.
His pants got dirty.
His shirt got dirty.
It was a dirty job.

He spent many, many minutes looking for the earring.

The other boy, however, wasn't helping.
He watched his friend and frowned.

The girl, meanwhile, just stood there.
No way was she getting dirty.

Finally, the boy found the earring!

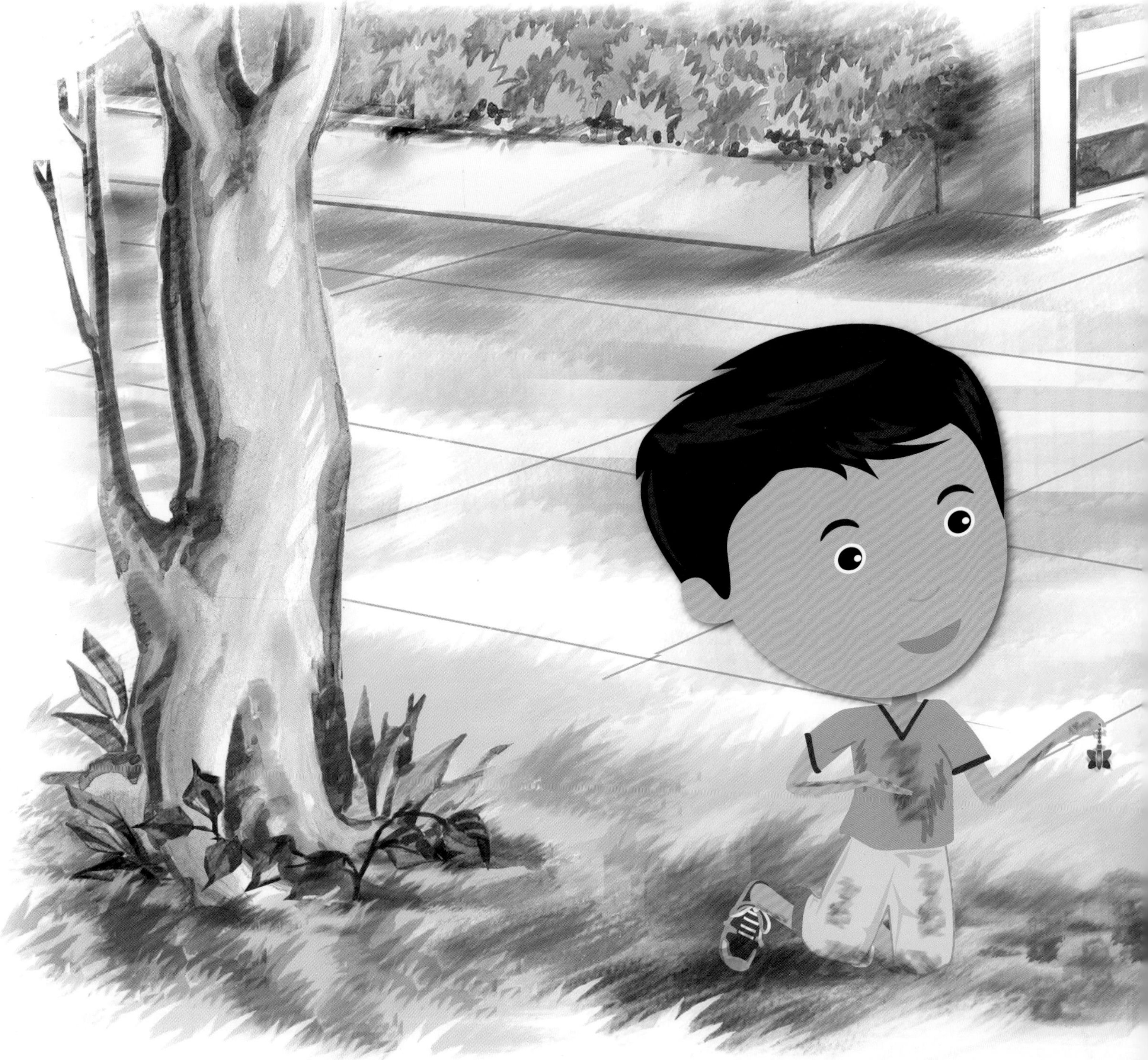

He picked it up and dusted it off.
With a gentle smile, he handed it to the girl.

She quickly grabbed the earring and yelled at the boy,

"Give me my earring! You're getting it dirty!"

She stormed away.
   She didn't say, "Thank you."
She still seemed angry.

The boy who found the earring
shrugged his shoulders and smiled.

He looked at his friend and said cheerfully, "Come on, let's play!"

The other boy played for a while,
but he wasn't having fun.
He was upset about something.

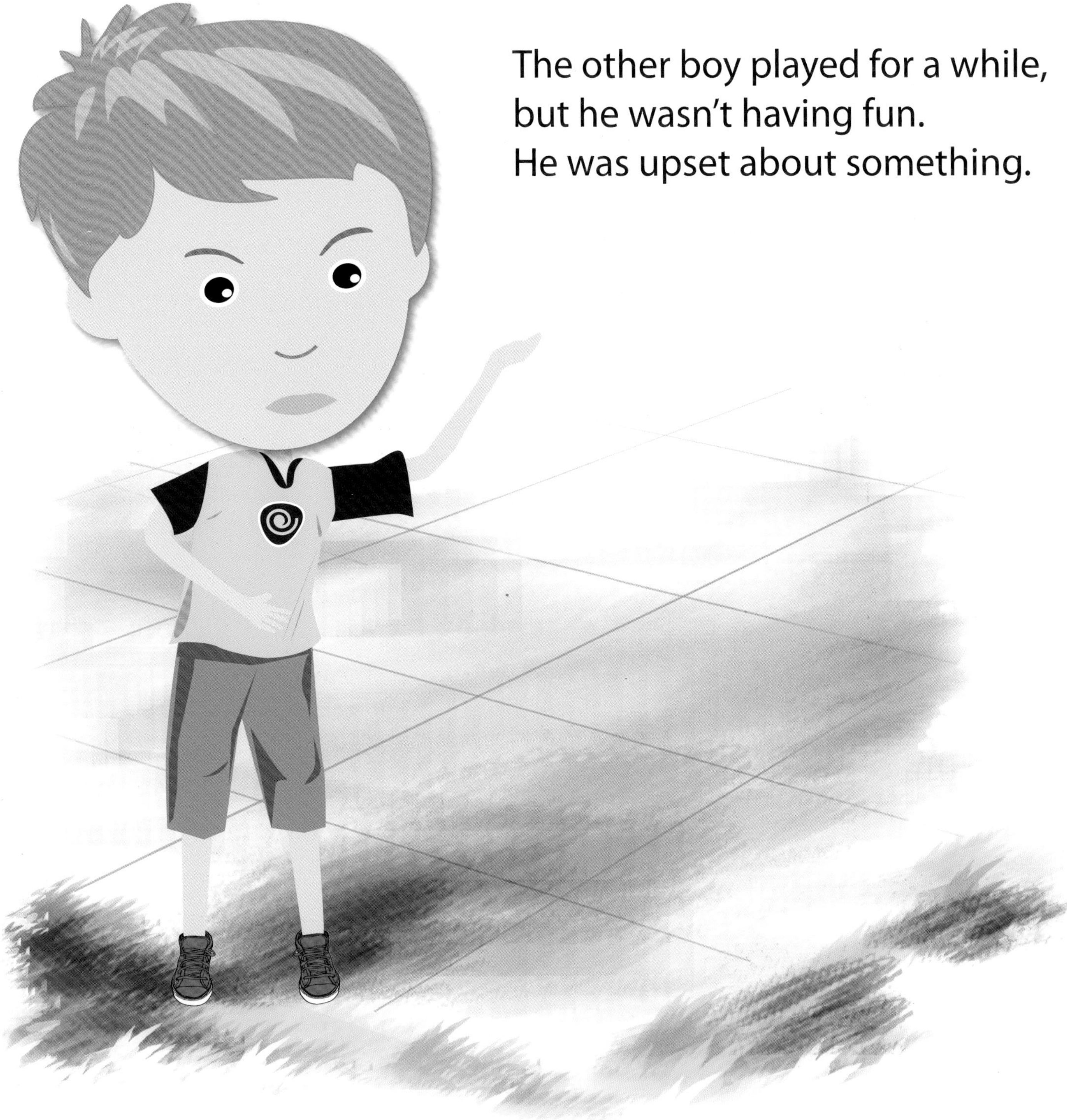

Finally, he said to his friend, "That girl was so mean! She's always like that. You found her earring and then she just yelled at you. She didn't even say, 'Thank you.'"

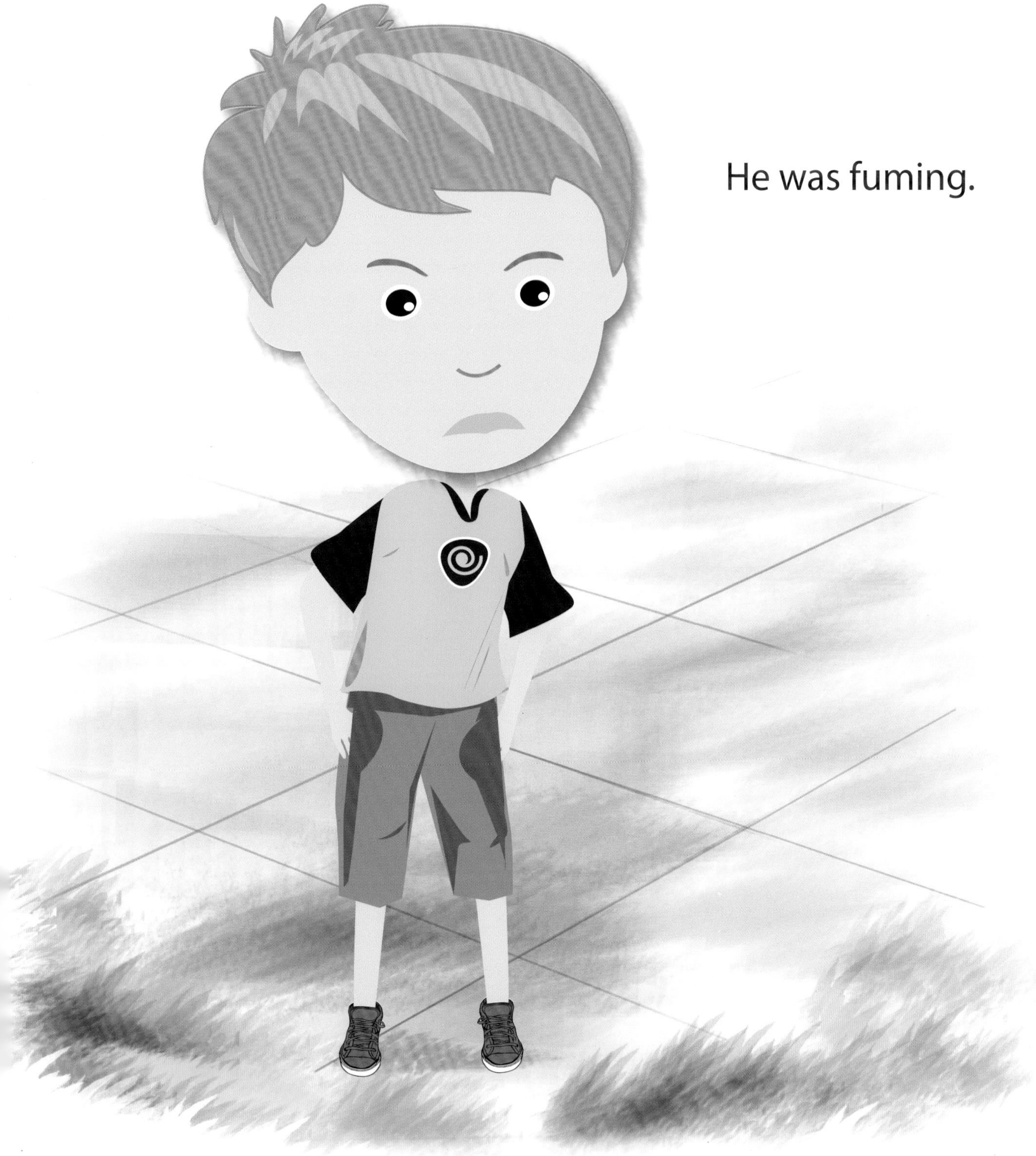

He was fuming.

The boy who found the earring
looked at his friend kindly.

He said, "Hey, buddy, are you
still thinking about that earring?
I gave it to that girl a while ago,
and now she's gone.
It's a beautiful day.
We could be playing and having fun,
right here and right now.

Why are you **Still There?**"

A Brief Explanation

Hi Kids! Did you know this story is based on an ancient Zen fable? In the fable, a monk carries a not-so-nice princess across a muddy waterhole, while his friend gets upset over the situation and has trouble letting it go. It's a very old and beautiful story, but the ideas and lessons are just as important in today's world.

So, why do you think the wise boy in our story doesn't get frustrated by the girl? Here are some of our ideas . . .

We often do things in life because we want something in return. We are nice to someone because we want that person to say, "Thank you," or to be nice back to us. But, when the other person isn't thankful, or is even rude, we get upset. And as we think about it, we get even more upset.

In this story, the wise boy finds the girl's earring because he wants to help. Nothing more, nothing less. He doesn't try to find that earring because he wants the girl to be nice to him. He doesn't look because he wants her to say, "Thank you." He just looks. He doesn't think about how the girl will react. And after the girl is mean to the wise boy, he simply lets it go.

His friend, however, focuses on that experience and keeps thinking about it. Does that extra thinking change anything? Does it make the girl nicer? No, it doesn't. But while that boy stews in his frustration, his wise friend moves on and is ready to play again. The wise boy is in the moment, and he isn't letting a past negative event bring him down.

These are just a few ways to interpret the story. What are your ideas?

can you find the matching earrings?